DRIVE LIKE HELL

AN AUTUMN FROST STORY

JESSE FRESCO

First published by Seven Starfighters Publishing 2026
Copyright © 2026 by Jesse Fresco

This novel is entirely a work of fiction. The names, characters, and incidents portrayed in it are the work of the author's imagination. Any resemblance to actual persons, living or dead, events or localities is entirely coincidental.

Edited by Brian Paone
Interior Formatting by Kari Holloway
Cover Art and Formatting by Amy Hunter

ISBN: 979-8-9945954-0-4

"I should have read my horoscope this morning."

—Maindrian Pace, *Gone in 60 Seconds*

CHAPTER ONE

Autumn Frost was, begrudgingly, a TAF (To-and-From) driver in Annapolis, Maryland. She had taken the job after her previous employment had let her go due to the economic collapse around the United States. She used to be a welder; now she drove drunk college kids around town at night. It was by no means a bad job, and on good nights she could bring in a decent sum. But it wasn't what she wanted. When push came to shove though, want and need were two different things.

It was 5 p.m. on New Year's Eve. It was cold. So cold that she wondered if anyone would actually brave the night to celebrate the new year. Despite that, she needed to bring in some kind of income. It was infuriating that driving services in the US didn't offer holiday bonuses. However, with enough fares, it could easily make up for expenses. That said, she still sighed and groaned at the thought of spending her holiday working.

She was a big, tough woman—deep red hair, a muscular body, but a kind face. Over the last ten years as a welder, her body had toned and shaped itself. On top of that, she had a consistent workout routine which kept her from slipping into bad habits, such as excessive fast food or too much drinking. One of her favorite comedians, Doug Stanhope, once said, "If you own nothing else in this world, you own the fucking meat that hangs from your bones." It was true, and she refused to let such good meat go to waste.

She closed the door to her modest one-bedroom apartment and headed downstairs to begin her shift. The twenty-something year old building was well kept yet certainly needed renovation, but no one ever came to give the place a facelift. It was a simple brick and mortar exterior, with a drab beige interior through a security door. She didn't mind, as it suited her needs just fine. It was cheap.

As a fiscally conservative person, she always lived beneath her means. One emergency in America could bankrupt a person. Therefore, she kept her expenses low, saved whenever possible, and if anything was ever free, she would jump at the chance to take it, no matter what it was.

Autumn pushed open the heavy, squeaky entrance door to her building, and a wall of icy air punched her face like a brick. It was windy and stung like needles. She pressed hard on the door unlock button on her car keys and ran to the driver-side door of her Honda Accord. She flung open the door open, climbed in, and slammed it shut. The interior was just as brisk, but at least there was no wind. She turned over the engine and flipped on the heater, the heated seats, and the headlights. It was almost totally dark outside, the sun giving off its last few rays of light over the horizon. She rubbed her hands together to bring some warmth back to them. She hated winter.

Setting up for rides was easy enough. The app essentially did everything except the driving part. Sign up and register your vehicle. After that, ensure the vehicle was in tiptop shape. If it wasn't clean and efficient, TAF would reject it for service. A vehicle also had to maintain a very simple design—no elevated wheels, no under-glow kit. Plain Jane normal. Autumn's Honda perfectly fit the bill. Also, while not required, she had installed a dash camera for safety, just in case a rider wanted to get rowdy.

When she had registered several months ago, the TAF app showed the best times for rides, which were early morning and late at night. Holidays were also extremely busy. As a single and frugal woman, New Year's Eve was the honey pot to start the new year. *New year, new me,* she thought. *Or whatever.* She had told herself that several times through the last three years, but she seemed to be stuck. Coasting through life. Day in, day out. Like many people's new year's resolutions, the reality of the world would break them, and life would continue as normal. Starting this new year, she felt that something had to change—something exciting needed to happen.

One way or another, the new year had to bring about a new Autumn Frost.

She flipped on the app and checked the ride calls. Even at 5 p.m., the town of Annapolis was already bustling, people settling into their favorite watering holes to count down to the new year. She would admire them from her driver's seat.

She shifted into Reverse, backed out of her parking space, shifted into Drive, and turned onto the highway.

Her first call was a couple from Arnold that was headed to Stan and Joe's tavern on West Street. Autumn turned right down Arnold Road, which then branched off to Severn Way. She scanned the houses, found the correct one, and parked to the side. As she began texting, the boyfriend and girlfriend exited their house—both wearing jeans and black and purple Baltimore Ravens hoodies.

The rear passenger door opened, and the girlfriend entered first.

Autumn asked, "Trevor?"

"Yup, that's me," Trevor answered. "And this is Maggie."

"How's your day going?" Maggie asked.

"I just started, so I'll let you know later tonight," Autumn jested. "And hey, go Ravens."

The couple cheered, *"Go Ravens!"* Then they buckled their seatbelts.

Stan and Joe's was by no means far away, but it was far enough to justify highway safety. Autumn shifted into Drive again, pulled a U-turn, and headed toward the highway. As she drove, she flipped on a top-forty playlist to fill the dead air. It was always awkward in the car without conversation.

As the music played, Trevor asked, "Is your name really Autumn Frost?"

"Yes, it is."

"Isn't that a flower?"

"It was my mom's favorite. Her surname was already Frost, so she saw an opportunity."

"That's a very pretty name," Maggie added.

"Thank you."

Autumn turned right onto Governor Ritchie Highway and slowly merged into the traffic. Her black Honda melded in with the rest of the drab vehicles headed to who-knew-where.

Trevor continued. "You gonna be driving all night?"

"Probably. It'll depend whether I meet my goal for tonight."

A red mustang sped past Autumn's Honda and darted between traffic as they headed toward the Severn River Bridge. Under her breath, she whispered, "Asshole."

"Why do people do that?" Maggie asked.

"Do what?" Autumn replied.

"Speed through traffic like that. Like, what difference does it make if you get there ten minutes from now or five minutes? So stupid."

"Some people are always in a hurry. I think it's better to get there when you get there."

"Sounds very Zen," Trevor said.

"Eh, just sensible, I think. Was never really one for philosophy."

They crossed the bridge onto Baltimore Blvd., turned left at King George Street, and continued toward College Avenue. Traffic picked up as they approached town, and they ended up stopping at every red light. Bumper-to-bumper vehicles crowed the road, several of them also TAF drivers making their rounds. *Tis' the season*, Autumn thought.

Finally, after an excessive amount of stop-and-start, Autumn rounded the center point of downtown, Church Circle. In the middle of Church Circle was St. Anne's Episcopal Church, which had stood there for hundreds of years. While it was a functioning church, it was also a historic piece of tourism, with a clock tower and a surrounding black iron fence. Autumn had driven past the large, brick church innumerable times but had never gone inside. She was an atheist and feared she might catch on fire should she walk through the doors.

The Honda came to the second turn off from the circle and was finally on West Street—the main thoroughfare. Lined on both sides by historic buildings, it was a popular spot for food, drinks, and live music. It was partially paved, partially cobblestone, but always felt like a tapestry of old America. Even the newer restaurants felt older and outdated by the standards of gentrification. The coffee shop on the right-hand side of the street looked the same as their destination, Stan and Joe's, on the left-hand side of the street. Same build, same architecture.

Autumn eased on the brakes and slowed to a crawl. Pedestrians crossing randomly with no regard for personal safety or traffic laws. As they approached the bar, she pulled over and turned on her hazards. "Here you go," Autumn said. "Have fun tonight."

Maggie opened the rear driver-side door and stepped out. "We will. Maybe we'll see you again later."

"We'll see."

"Thank you," Trevor added as he followed Maggie out of the rear driver-side door. He closed the door, and the pair jogged across the street to avoid the oncoming traffic.

Autumn marked her ride as complete, and as she checked the local request list, she received her first tip of the night. For a thirty-four-dollar ride, Trevor had sent an eight-dollar tip, slightly higher than 20 percent. She smirked while searching for her next fare.

For the next three and a half hours, she drove people from various places to and from the city. People from all the neighboring cities, such as Davidsonville, Edgewater, Stevensville, Mayo. Single people, couples, groups. It was a busy night, and by 9 p.m., she had met her quota. She could call it a night, log off, and head home, but the carrot of a little extra cash dangled before her. If it was busy between 5 p.m. and 9 p.m., the rest of the night would be twice as good. She decided to take a short break, then get back on the road.

She pulled into a parking lot off Housely Road and went into a good and cheap noodle restaurant—just the way she liked it. She used the restroom, then ordered her favorite ramen while she cleared some emails and messages. Most of it was junk, but one was from her old employer, asking if she would be willing to return to her old position at half her salary. She felt insulted reading that message and deleted it. While being a TAF driver wasn't exactly giving her the same level of income that her welding position had several years prior, returning to it with half the pay would put her in an even lower position than she currently was. She shook her head in bitter disappointment.

America had become nothing but an Ayn Randian nightmare. It was hustle or be hustled. Autumn hated it and yearned for a better life, one away from America. If she had the money, she would jet overseas and live out the rest of her days in somewhere nice, like Denmark or Finland—anywhere but America.

She sucked in the last string of noodles, slurped down the broth, and headed out. She climbed into her driver's seat… and then just sat. She didn't open the app; she didn't play on her phone. Just stared out the window and tried to zone out. *This is no way to live*, Autumn thought. Part of her wanted to cry; part of her wanted to scream. She knew she was better than this. She knew that given the chance, she could rise above her current situation and have a better life.

But the world had other plans, and they didn't involve Autumn Frost.

She exhaled sharply and grabbed her phone. Just as she was about to open the TAF app, she flipped to her messages. She scrolled down and saw her ex-girlfriend Becky's last message. It had ended badly several months earlier, but Autumn couldn't bring herself to delete the text thread. She scrolled up to the last five minutes of conversation between them and reread the thread for the hundredth time.

> BECKY: *You could go back to school and try to get something else.*
>
> AUTUMN: *You need money to do that, and I'm still struggling since I got fired.*
>
> B: *You're always struggling. You work all the time just to eke out a living.*
>
> A: *That's not fair.*
>
> B: *It's not fair to me that we still don't have a better place to live.*
>
> A: *The economy is bad right now. It'll pick up.*
>
> B: *You said that last time. And the time before. This is just the way that it is. We could live a decent life if you tried harder. I'm trying harder with more shifts at the hospital.*
>
> A: *I'm so tired of fighting about this.*
>
> B: *Me too. I gotta go.*

The conversation ended there. Autumn hadn't been able to bring herself to reply. When she had arrived home that night, Becky was gone. Then she had cried herself to sleep.

Autumn thought hard about sending another message. Enough time had passed. Maybe they could reconcile. Maybe things would be okay. Maybe, maybe, maybe.

Then she closed the thread. She had spent too long off the clock, and the night was rolling on. Right when she opened the TAF app, she got a request not far down the road. She selected it, shifted into gear, and pulled out.

Autumn turned left, and then immediately left again onto Generals Highway. Traffic was dense, but thankfully, it was green lights the whole way. She turned left again onto Knollwood Drive, followed the windy road up and down a series of small hills, and stopped in front of a nice two-story home, like the ones depicted in '80s and '90s sitcoms. Back then, houses like that were very affordable. Now they cost around half a million dollars.

Autumn texted the rider that she had arrived and waited. And waited.

No one came outside.

A few lights were on in the house, but it was mostly dark.

Autumn texted again.

No reply, though the customer had seen the message.

Just as she was about to call the number, the rear passenger door flung open, and a woman with a large backpack darted inside. She slammed the door, locked it, and yelled, "Drive!"

"Uh, are you Cassie?" Autumn asked.

"Yes! Just drive!"

A tall man, with curly brown hair, emerged from the darkness, dashed toward the Honda, and reached for the passenger-side handle. Fuming with rage, he screamed, "*Get the fuck out here, right now! Give it back!*"

"Drive!" Cassie screamed again.

The curly haired man reached behind his back and pulled out a .38 snub-nosed pistol.

Autumn slammed on the accelerator and sped away as a single shot fired with a loud pop. The bullet zinged wide and hit nothing. The Honda sped over the next hill, and the curly haired man disappeared from her rearview mirror. The engine roared as they weaved around turn after turn. Autumn checked her GPS and noticed a serious problem; the street was about to dead end.

The GPS said with a soft woman's voice, "Please turn around."

In the back seat, Cassie exclaimed, "Oh no."

The street finally dead ended with a cul-de-sac. She made a wide U-turn and faced back down the road she had just come from. With only one way out, she realized what they would have to do: drive straight back toward the man with the gun.

Autumn exhaled and thought, *Okay, this could be bad.*

Chapter Two

The engine purred softly as the Honda sat still in the center of the cul-de-sac. Autumn's heart pounded so hard that it felt as though it would burst from her chest.

Cassie leaned forward and clasped the headrest of the front passenger seat, her backpack laying in her lap.

Autumn glanced at Cassie in the rearview mirror, then at the bag, then back to Cassie. Whatever they were caught up in, Autumn figured that was probably the reason. *Give it back*, the man had yelled.

And the night had started out so well.

"Are you hurt?" Autumn asked, craning her head around.

"No," Cassie responded, with a whimper in her voice. Her hands wouldn't stop shaking.

"Okay. There's only one way out, so I need you to stay down. Okay?"

"We can't go back that way!"

"Unless you know how to fly, this is the only way out. Just get down, stay down. Understand? And while you're at it, call the cops."

"No! No police!"

"Why?"

Cassie said nothing. She looked as if she was ready to burst into tears.

"Fine. But when we're out of here, we're gonna have words. Just hang on!"

Cassie cowered as low as possible and curled into a ball. She wrapped her arms around the backpack, as if holding onto it so tightly created a level of security. She closed her eyes and braced herself for the movement of the car.

Autumn closed her eyes, exhaled once, twice, three times. Then she shifted the car into Drive and mashed the accelerator. *New year, new me*, she thought.

The car peeled around the bends as they retraced their route toward the mouth of the neighborhood. Autumn hit 50 mph in the 35-mph zone by the time they were in sight of the house that Cassie had darted from. She hoped the gunman would be gone before they went passed but no such luck. He was keying the lock on a decade-old Range Rover when he saw Autumn's headlights streak across his view.

In a panic, Autumn flashed her high beams as fast as possible to create a strobe effect that would hopefully blind the gunman long enough for them escape. As they soared past the house, Autumn heard several high-pitched pop-pop-pop sounds over the roar of her engine. The last pop was followed by a zing sound.

Autumn ducked down as she accelerated to 60 mph and raced down the cold blacktop road.

*****

They pulled into one of the parking garages at Westfield Mall and followed the ramp to the rooftop deck. They emerged into the night to see only a few scattered cars.

Icy streetlamps illuminated the beige concrete and blocked the starlight. Autumn pulled the car into the farthest spot from the ramp. Except for her and Cassie's breathing, the world was totally silent. Everyone was out, getting ready to celebrate the new year.

Finally, Autumn softly said, "You can get up now."

With a pensive stare, Autumn watched Cassie's reflection rise into the rearview mirror.

The terrified girl swallowed hard. "Thank you."

Autumn, in a rage, unbuckled her seatbelt, flung open her car door, and stepped out to check for any damage. Plumes of icy breath streamed from her mouth and nostrils as she circled her vehicle. Finally, she saw what she was expecting—a single bullet hole in the driver's side trunk lid. "*Fuck!*" She crouched and stared at the concrete, running her hands through her hair. She realized then that she was sweating and that her hair was damp.

Cassie gradually opened the rear driver's side door and silently watched Autumn.

Autumn slowly raised her head and glared at Cassie. She stood, rushed toward Cassie, and reached into the back seat to grab the backpack. Cassie fought back, clamping down hard and twisting from Autumn.

"What's in the bag? Give it to me," Autumn yelled.

"No! I can't!"

Autumn grabbed both of Cassie's ankles and yanked Cassie from the car. The girl dropped to the frozen ground, landing on her back, with a loud smack; the backpack was still wrapped in her arms. Autumn straddled Cassie's waist, jerked back her right arm, and balled her fist, ready to strike. The frightened girl cowered again, hyperventilating from the drop punching the air out her lungs. Autumn gritted her teeth, so sure of herself not ten seconds earlier. Now she couldn't bring herself to hit a scared, young girl who was clearly a victim.

Autumn released her punch at nothing but air and wandered to the edge of the parking deck. She placed her palms flat atop the wall, feeling the cold, rough concrete. It was so cold that it hurt, but she was too angry to care. She surveyed the road below. No cars drove by. The world felt lifeless.

Cassie slowly composed herself and got to her feet. She ran her arms through the straps of the backpack and crossed her arms. She was only wearing jeans and a black long sleeve shirt, not nearly enough to resist the December night. Cassie's teeth chattered in the cold.

Autumn wore almost the same as Cassie, jeans with her red Maryland Terrapin's hoodie. She hadn't been expecting to get out of her car during her shift, let alone be involved in a shooting, car chase, and whatever else the night had yet to bring.

With a sharp sigh, Autumn turned around. "I'm sorry."

Cassie said nothing.

"I need you to tell me what's in the bag."

Cassie said nothing.

"Okay, fine." Autumn marched to her car and got into the driver's seat. "You're on your own, kid." She slammed the car door and started the engine.

Cassie rushed forward, and through her shivers and chattering teeth, she screamed, "No! Please don't leave me!"

Autumn quickly reversed, then screeched away, leaving Cassie behind. With crossed arms, Cassie chased after the car, pleading and screaming. Autumn didn't look back and turned onto the down ramp of the parking deck.

Then she stopped.

She paused and finally craned her head to see the girl in the distance.

Cassie stood frozen and alone under the bright white lights. She crouched and curled up, trying her best to keep the heat from escaping her body.

Autumn, annoyed that she wasn't totally heartless, lightly shook her head and said to herself, "Goddammit." She shifted into Reverse and retraced her path toward Cassie. "New year, new me."

The car stopped a few feet to Cassie's left. Autumn reached back to open the rear passenger-side door, exposing Autumn's highly annoyed face. "Get in. You'll freeze to death out there."

Cassie jumped up and climbed into the back seat, then slammed the door. Her teeth chattered so quickly that her jaw almost sounded like she was crushing pebbles. She rubbed her hands together and hunched her shoulders forward, trying to get warm again. Autumn turned the heater on high and blasted it into the back seat. Cassie held up her hands and felt the rush of hot air across her fingertips—a relief from the biting cold. Her fingers loosened as blood flowed back into them.

"You're welcome," Autumn said with half-closed eyes. She was annoyed with herself. Her night was officially ruined, her car had an extra hole in it, and she was now the de facto guardian of a scared, young girl who was involved in God knew what. But she couldn't bring herself to just leave. Too many times, she had just given up in the past. This time had to be different. "If you want me to help you, you need to help me," Autumn continued.

"I don't think I should tell you much. I just need you to drive me somewhere."

"We don't move until I know what you're involved in. I was just shot at tonight, so that very clearly means I'm as involved as you are." Autumn turned around and got right in Cassie's face. "So do not bullshit me. What am I involved in?"

Cassie sat quiet for a few moments, like a child whose furious parent had scolded them. Then, sheepishly, she said, "It was just supposed to be a couple vials. That was all."

"What?"

"Max said it was just a little bit. He didn't say it was two whole pounds."

"Is Max the guy who shot at us?"

"Yeah."

"Wild guess. It's drugs, isn't it?"

Cassie said nothing.

"What kind?"

"Fentanyl."

"Great." Autumn rubbed her eyes, suddenly very tired.

"This was more than I was expecting."

"Yeah, I agree," Autumn said with vexation.

"I'm sorry. I panicked. I locked myself in the bathroom, then climbed out the window when you arrived. He was kicking in the door when I ran to the car. I didn't know what else to do. I said it was too much. Someone would come looking."

And there it was. It finally clicked for Autumn. "Wait. You're saying this stash isn't yours... or his. It's stolen."

"Yeah." Cassie buried her face in her hands in shame.

"Oh, fuck my life." Autumn started to get a headache.

"I'm sorry," Cassie cried out, her voice breaking. Then tears streamed down her face.

Autumn flipped the heater to a lower setting to dull the noise. She had to think. A young girl on the run, with a stash of stolen fent, was in her back seat. A conundrum, indeed. Autumn weighed her options. Cassie had said no police, for obvious reasons. Even doing a good deed of turning her in to protect her from Max would result in jail time. And with the government having declared fentanyl as a weapon of mass destruction, Cassie would face heavy prison time. Who knew how long she had been hustling fent? Or the better question…

"Are you using?" Autumn asked.

"No! Not fent. Just… other stuff." She went quiet.

Autumn sighed. "Okay." She canceled the ride on her phone app.

Cassie's phone pinged with the notification. "What… what are you doing?" Cassie whimpered.

"You get a free ride tonight. Where did the fent come from?"

"You wanna return it?"

"It's that, or I can drop you off at county. Your choice."

Cassie got the message. She wiped away her tears and rubbed her nose. A dribble of snot landed on her pants. "Okay."

"Okay. So… who does it belong to?"

"There's a guy in Mayo. On Turkey Point Island. Max took it from him. He runs an operation on the island."

Autumn had never been to Turkey Point Island, but the name was familiar. It was an oasis of modest to upscale homes on the edge of Chesapeake Bay. A fentanyl den operating from such a modest area was odd and a bit farfetched. "Seems a bit out of the way for trafficking, isn't it?"

"It comes in from the Navy yard, and then runners move it down there. The whole thing is run from one of the houses on Turkey Point. It's all brought in by servicemen looking for a side hustle."

Autumn nodded. "I guess that makes sense. Navy men get it overseas, bring it back here, and pass it off outside the base. That's actually kind of brilliant. Guessing Max is Navy, huh?"

Cassie sniffled loudly. "Yeah. He lives off base though. Said if we sold the stuff ourselves, we could go anywhere we want."

Autumn retrieved a wad of tissues from her armrest and handed them to woman in the back seat.

Cassie quickly snatched them from Autumn's hand and blew her nose. She wiped away a few more tears and swallowed hard.

Autumn tapped the steering wheel with a soft rhythm—*tap, tap, tap*—as she considered what to do. "Fuck it." She opened her GPS. "Give me the address."

"No, wait. We can't return it!"

"Why not?"

"Because… Max shot one of their guys when he stole it. Even if they got the bag back, they'd still be after us. We can't just give it back. They'll kill me."

"They don't know where you live, do they?"

Cassie said nothing.

That means yes, Autumn thought. "Look, you don't really have much of a choice. Either you return it and hope for the best or you go to federal prison. Up to you."

Cassie sat still for a moment and sniffled again. "Okay. Let's go. Maybe I can do a trade with them."

"Trade what?"

"I give them the drugs and tell them where to find Max. Maybe they'll let me go."

Two birds, one stone, Autumn thought.

"All right, let's do it." She pulled up her GPS. "Where to?"

"3733 Upton Road."

Autumn entered the address. "Twenty minutes away. Sit back. We'll be there before you know it."

"Thank you."

"Don't mention it. And I mean that; don't mention it. Buckle up."

Cassie sat behind Autumn and secured her seatbelt. Autumn shifted into Drive and slowly pulled toward the down ramp. She turned right as they casually descended to the level below.

Then she slammed on the brakes and stopped.

The Range Rover from before screeched to a stop on the opposite side of the parking deck, having just come up the ramp. It was too far to see the driver, but who else would be ascending a deserted parking deck outside Westfield Mall on New Year's Eve? It was Max. Had to be.

Cassie leaned forward, her face right next to Autumn's, as she studied the Range Rover in the distance. They both were aghast by the sudden stroke of more bad luck.

"How the fuck…" Autumn said, her voice trailing off. *You just had to have a heart, didn't you, Autumn?*

Chapter Three

The two vehicles stared each other down. Neither moved. Plumes of white smoke puffed from the Range Rover's exhaust pipe. The bright, artificial glass tubes on the ceiling lit everything perfectly all around. No shadows anywhere.

Cassie's phone buzzed. She answered.

"Give it back, bitch!" Max yelled. "I ain't gonna ask again! Give it back!"

"Give me the phone," Autumn said.

With her skinny fingers trembling, Cassie handed Autumn the phone.

"We already called the cops," Autumn said. "They're on the way."

"Who the fuck is this?"

"There's only two people in this car. Who do you think it is? I'm the Dalai Lama."

"Toss the bag out, and you can leave."

"And Cassie?"

"None of your fucking business, cunt. Toss it."

"Sorry, she already paid for her ride. I'm on the clock."

The line went dead. The Range Rover shifted into gear and surged toward Autumn and Cassie.

Autumn shifted into Reverse. "Get down!" Autumn slammed on the accelerator, twisted the steering wheel, and sped up the ramp in reverse, using her rear camera to track her trajectory to the top deck.

The Range Rover accelerated as it rounded the corner and raced up the ramp.

Once again, out in the cold, bitter night, Autumn kept her foot on the accelerator as the menace in front of her gained distance. The two vehicles raced across the rooftop, and just before the deck dead ended, Autumn spun the steering wheel hard left. She was now parallel with the guardrail and reduced her speed to regain control. The Range Rover slammed on its brakes and turned to follow Autumn.

As Autmn drove in reverse, Max lowered his driver-side window and stuck out the .38 snub-nose. Autumn's eyes widened, and she spun the steering wheel hard to the left again just as he fired a shot. The bullet pierced the guardrail beyond Autumn's car as she zoomed out of its path.

Out of options, Autumn yelled, "Hang on!" She spun the steering wheel a hundred and eighty degrees, and the car spun loudly in a semicircle on the rooftop. She quickly shifted to Drive, slammed on the gas pedal, and sped forward like a racehorse hearing the starting pistol. The engine roared as she sped toward the down ramp again, but she took the corner way too fast. For a split second, the car elevated onto two wheels as she rounded the railing and entered the down ramp. The two airborne wheels quickly found traction again and settled onto the concrete with a loud thump.

The Range Rover maintained the pursuit and turned the corner to follow. Max aimed again, fired, but, once again, missed. Max fired round after round but hit nothing.

As Autumn reached the bottom deck, she noticed the shooting had stopped and checked her rearview mirror. "Out of rounds, aren't you?" She accelerated and sped through the parking exit. She bounced onto the blacktop, fish tailed left for a second, then regained control as she headed east.

The Range Rover gave chase down the two-way street as it exited the garage. Autumn stayed on the correct side, while the Range Rover accelerated and veered into the opposite lane. They became parallel for a split second before Autumn pulled hard right toward the stoplight at the end of main entrance road. The Range Rover slammed on its brakes, turned a sharp right, and mounted the curb for a moment to get back on Autumn's tail.

As Autumn sped forward, she noticed the stoplight was red, and some traffic still passed through the intersection. She slammed on her brakes, swerved into the right lane, and took a right on the red. The car lurched left as she rounded the corner, and a car just behind her blared its horn as she cut off someone. The Range Rover fell in behind the cut-off car, zipped around it, and kept going after Autumn and Cassie.

In the reflection of her rearview mirror, Autumn noticed Max still hot on her tail. She turned left and entered a small shopping center with some fast-food restaurants and convenience stores. She cut through the minuscule parking lot and reentered traffic on the opposite side of the road.

Max slammed on his brakes and pulled a U-turn in the middle of traffic. A pair of sedans skidded to a stop as Max looped around and kept up with the chase. One sedan popped the curb, hit a light pole, and stalled out. The Range Rover gained speed again.

"We gotta get off this road," Autumn said. "You still okay?"

"Yes," Cassie yelled.

"All right, let's take a detour." Autumn accelerated and eased into a soft right turn toward Route 50—one of the largest and busiest highway systems in the United States. She turned onto the on-ramp and pressed harder on the gas pedal. Her car was like a bullet firing from a gun as she slid into traffic on the highway. The road was much more packed than she expected for New Year's Eve. Not a good place to escape.

She glanced in her rearview to see Max still following. "This motherfucker," she groaned. "You have terrible taste in men, you know that?"

Cassie said nothing, as she was still hunkered down, hiding.

Traffic was congested as Autumn sped in the center lane toward the next exit, with Max following just behind. She spotted a small gap between cars. The exit was approaching fast, so she would have to make her move. Only a hundred feet away, she darted between the two cars and slid out of traffic, entered the off-ramp, and escaped the highway. Max, trapped behind another vehicle, overshot the exit and was stuck on Route 50, heading away from Autumn and Cassie.

The off-ramp rose and rounded left toward the opposite side of the highway before descending onto Route 665 toward Riva. The chase was over.

Autumn drove a little farther and descended a second off-ramp to leave 665. She slowly turned right at a four-way intersection connected to the overpass of 665. This brought her onto Riva Road, a four-lane connecting street that led into the suburbs outside of town. She continued, stopped at a three-way intersection, turned left, and accelerated.

The pair of women found themselves in a small hotel district, with three-star hotels and parking lots that seemed much too large for the hotel capacity. She entered one of the lots and parked toward the back tree line. She killed the engine and sat in silence, realizing how loud her heart was pounding. Adrenaline still rushed through her body, and her hands shook.

"Okay, we're safe now," Autumn said. She exhaled sharply.

Cassie uncurled herself but kept herself low, out of sheer paranoia.

"It's okay. We lost him on the highway," Autumn followed up. *But how the fuck did he find us?* "Give me your phone."

Cassie handed over her phone.

Autumn swiped up and checked the settings. The GPS location tracker was set to On, and someone had recently pinged it. "Fuck," Autumn whispered. She swiped it to Off but wasn't sure if they had hidden a tracker on the phone too. She knew as much about cellphones as anyone, which was just enough to get them to work, but not *how* they worked. She opened the door and chucked the phone into the tree line.

"Hey, what the fuck," Cassie yelled.

"He was tracking you. That's how he found us in the garage. He doesn't have my phone number, so we're safe now."

"Oh."

"I'll buy you a new one, kid. Better this way."

"I thought we were gonna die."

"Yeah, well, sometimes you get lucky. Fasten your seatbelt. We'll get back on the road to Turkey Point."

Autumn turned over the engine, reversed, and navigated onto the road toward Edgewater, which connected to Mayo. The Annapolis area, for all its history, was a collection of small, nondescript towns interlocked with each other, with no real border or boundary between them beyond some vague lines on a map that no one bothered to look at. If someone said they were from Annapolis, that could just as easily mean they were from Mayo, or Davidsonville, or Severna Park. For many, to say they were from the Annapolis area was a point of pride for Marylanders. It was the heart of Maryland and much nicer than its more popular northern city of Baltimore.

The hotel district road wound around in an S-shape and ended at another three-way intersection on Solomons Island Road. Autumn turned right and merged with the traffic toward the South River Bridge. Traffic in this direction was light; everyone was still headed in the opposite direction toward town for the New Year's parties. As they rolled onto the bridge, Autumn checked her fuel gauge. She was down to a quarter of a tank. Not wanting to risk getting into another chase with a low tank, she figured it would be best to refuel. As they passed Coconut Joe's—a surf and turf restaurant—on the left, she said, "Gonna stop for gas. Just stay down. You want me to get you a water or anything?"

"A Coke, please."

"Okay."

They turned into the pump area for one of the three gas stations at a three-way intersection. As she stepped into the frosty night to fill the tank, she thought, *Why would anyone use the other two gas stations if this one is cheaper?* She let the thought go, not wanting to debate with herself about the nature of capitalism after such a rough night.

The handle clicked. Autumn returned the hose to the nozzle boot and headed into the convenience store attached to the station. Inside, she grabbed a Coke for Cassie and an energy drink for herself. Now coming down from the adrenaline rush, she felt herself crashing. She paid the bill and headed to the car.

Autumn handed the Coke to Cassie as she slid into the driver's seat. They cracked open their drinks, took big gulps, and let out long exhales. "So, that's your boyfriend, huh?" Autumn asked.

"What, where?" Cassie began, spinning around, paranoid.

"He's not around us, kid. I just mean in general."

"Oh. Yeah, that was Max." She took another gulp of drink.

"You don't really seem like the type to do this kind of stuff."

"He would bring me along on his runs. He said he was saving up to take us somewhere. Get us out of the country. He hasn't really cut it very well in the Navy, so they were planning to kick him out."

"Which means no retirement and dishonorable discharge. That's a bad look for trying to get a job in the future."

"Yeah, so he started doing this, fell in with some people, and I tagged along. It was easy money."

"How the fuck do you end up with someone like that?"

"I mean… I was young and stupid, I guess."

"Well, you're still young, but hopefully a little less stupid now."

Cassie said nothing.

"Are you high right now?"

Cassie said nothing.

"What did you take earlier?"

"I mean, I mainly do pills, but there's also Adderall and some coke sometimes. Max tried to get me to take harder stuff. That was when the fighting started."

"He was trying to dope you up so you would stay forever."

Cassie said nothing.

"Look, kid." Autumn turned to face Cassie. "You fucked up, and you're paying for it. This is a really big fucking mess, okay? Don't run from it; just own it. You fucked up. Say it."

"I fucked up."

"Good. Now what do you wanna do?"

"Fix it, I guess."

Autumn sighed. "Good enough." She faced forward again.

Just as she was about to start the engine, a pair of black pickup trucks, with tinted windows and spewing black exhaust, pulled into the station and stopped behind Autumn's car. No one stepped out. She sat still, frozen, and stared at the pair of monstrous vehicles in the rearview mirror.

The driver's side doors on both trucks opened simultaneously and out stepped two enormous men armed with handguns.

Autumn turned over the engine and sped from the station. Shots rang out, barely missing her car. Windows on the store exploded as bullets blasted through them, and one bullet ripped through one of the stations' fuel pumps. Gasoline erupted like a geyser.

Autumn sped down the back road behind a shopping center to avoid the traffic light. She crossed into a grocery store parking lot and maneuvered through parked cars to escape onto Riva Road. "Who *the fuck* are these guys?"

In her rearview mirror, she saw the two trucks give chase.

"*Who are they?*" Autumn yelled again.

"Might be the guy who Max stole the fent from."

Autumn turned left out the parking lot and found herself lucky that the stoplight was already green as she darted onto the road. "Fuck it. Toss the bag. They want it, right?"

"I can't! It's the only thing that I can trade now. I gotta give it back to the guy at Turkey Point."

"Just do it."

"I can't!"

The trucks turned left through the intersection and accelerated to follow.

Autumn groaned. "I should have kept the clock running."

Chapter Four

The three vehicles sped down the highway and back across South River Bridge. The traffic was much heavier heading in that direction. Autumn bobbed and weaved around cars as the two behemoths gave chase. Cassie ducked once again and held her bag tight, her last bargaining chip. Autumn glimpsed her GPS and realized they were traveling in the opposite direction to reach Turkey Point Island. She cursed under her breath and refocused on the road. The engine roared loudly as they rounded the first bend of blacktop across the bridge.

The Honda cut in front of a large delivery truck and moved into the far-right lane. Autumn knew another on-ramp to Route 50 lay ahead. If she could use the traffic as a blockade, they could escape again, just like with Max. There was just one problem ahead: a red light at the three-way intersection and no time to stop.

Traffic poured in from the T-section of the three-way. There was no way to cross without hitting someone, and even if she got super lucky and didn't, the traffic camera would snap her pic and mail her a huge fine. She chanced a look at her GPS and saw a small road just before the intersection. She slammed on the brakes, cut hard right, and swerved onto a small road leading to a backroad neighborhood of two-story homes.

The road was a loop that would eventually lead to the main road, but it was enough to bypass the traffic light and maybe shake the two trucks off her tail.

As she gently turned left at the first bend, she looked back to see them still on her. She followed the road around and eventually reached the opposite side of the intersection. She darted into the traffic, raced up the small hill and through another stoplight that was already thankfully green, then merged into the downslope on-ramp onto Route 665. She slowed to match the casually moving traffic rounding the bend.

"Look behind us," Autumn said.

Cassie slowly raised her head and looked through the back window. She saw nothing. "No one's behind us."

Autumn released a long sigh and slowly merged into traffic on 665. "We'll loop around and head back toward Edgewater." The GPS reoriented itself and stated they were fifteen minutes from their destination. *Just fifteen minutes and it's over*, Autumn thought. *Then just head home—*

"They're back," Cassie yelled.

Autumn spotted the pickups in the rearview, gunning it full speed ahead and jets of black smoke spewing from their exhausts. "How the fuck did they catch up? They didn't see us go down the ramp!" She turned her head all the way around, glanced at Cassie, then at the bag. "Open the bag! It's gotta have a tracker or something on it."

"But we got rid of my phone."

"Not your phone. Something else. Open it and go through every pocket!"

Cassie unzipped the main section and dumped out the contents. Several plastic bags, stuffed to the brim with vials of fent, tumbled out and landed on the back seat. The bags rolled back and forth as Autumn swerved around cars on the highway. Cassie pawed through the inside and found nothing. She reached above her and pushed the button for the backseat overhead lamp to illuminate the bag's black canvas interior.

Their only option was to get back onto Route 50. The traffic and congestion could buy them time.

The road bent slightly to the right as it became a long on-ramp for Route 50. The road would eventually split into two directions—one headed onto Route 50, the other onto Route 97 toward Baltimore. It was beginning to feel like a Sisyphean feat trying to get to their destination. They were literally going in circles, hitting the same ramps, crossing through the same roadways.

"Did you find anything?" Autumn asked with annoyance.

"I'm still looking." Cassie had opened all the pockets on the front. Still nothing. She ran her fingers along the interior lining. Again, nothing. "There's nothing here."

"Open the bags. Check the vials."

"What?"

"Just do it!"

Cassie ripped open the plastic bags. More than twenty vials of fentanyl poured out, rolled around the back seat, and eventually fell to the floorboard, now rolling back and forth across the carpet. Cassie cursed loudly and checked each vial, setting aside the checked ones in the backpack.

Autumn merged left at the split onto Route 50 toward Washington DC. There were plenty of exits before then, but they were spaced far apart, and police speed traps were usually positioned along the road. The traffic was still heavy but not as bad as before.

The two trucks followed and merged in, one by one.

Cassie finished checking the last vial and found nothing. She carefully opened the second bag to keep it from ripping open like the last one and, once again, checked the vials. She eventually found one that had something inside. She held it up to the light and noticed it was a small circular disk with a blinking red light. "Got it!" She leaned on the armrest between the front seats and handed it to Autumn.

Autumn inspected it for a moment, lowered the window, then chucked it onto the highway. "All right, sit back and buckle up again. Gotta lose these guys." She slammed the gas pedal to the floor, and the engine roared like a lion. She had pushed her Honda many times before but never like that. She was surprised the engine wasn't on the verge of exploding.

The trucks were gaining, though. Their engines were built for power, and there was no way a Honda Accord would outmatch them. Autumn did what she could, dodging and juking through traffic, doing her best to prevent a collision. She knew it was risky to be on such a populated roadway, but, as they had passed the last turn off before exit 16, four miles down the road, there was no other option.

So, she pressed on and hoped for the best.

And then bad luck struck again.

Speed trap. Police lights. Hiding in the dark service road between the two sides of the highway. The red and blue lights blazed, turned onto Route 50, and joined the chase.

Autumn rolled her eyes and groaned. "*Fuuucccckkkkkkk!*"

*****

In the woods next to Route 50, a large and majestic ten-horned buck was foraging for the last remaining scraps of food before rejoining its pack for the night. It pitter-pattered across the crunchy leaves in the dark for anything that would be a late-night snack. As it plodding along, it spotted a patch of winterberries and decided to have its fill. One by one, it pecked them off the small bush's branches. Once it felt content, the deer sauntered down a small hillock toward a large black road with passing lights.

The buck had seen lights like these many times before and knew, through instinct, that it should avoid these bright things. It moseyed to the black road and stopped. The lights were sparse now, and the buck needed to reach the other side to get home. It slowly moved a few paces, then darted out. The buck reached the center of the road where a short stone wall separated the two sides of the moving lights. It hopped the wall and took the risk again. It was halfway across when a pair of lights rushed at it.

It stopped dead in its tracks, mesmerized by the growing set of circular beams.

*****

Autumn saw the red and blue lights trailing just behind the two trucks. Were she to stop, the trucks would catch up and take them out. If she kept going, eventually the trucks would overtake her and force her onto the shoulder. The night's options were becoming less appealing by the second.

The next exit was still two miles away.

Ahead, she saw the silhouette of a deer hop over the divider between the roadways. She moved into the far-right lane to avoid hitting it and maintained her speed. As she passed the deer, she watched it in her rearview mirror try to dart across the highway, then stop at the oncoming lights of one of the trucks.

The deer instantly exploded into an enormous geyser of blood and furry flesh. Sharp antlers from the decapitated buck flew toward the windshield of the first truck. It punched through the driver's side of the windshield and embedded into the glass. The driver panicked and swerved left and right before finally corkscrewing and tumbling the pickup onto its right side. It spun and flipped, then slid on its side. Hot orange sparks erupted from under the chassis as it slid like a bar of soap across molasses before coming to a stop.

The cruiser pulled to the shoulder to assess the damage, letting the second truck and Autumn drive away.

Two down, one to go.

The next exit appeared in the distance—exit 16 toward Davidsonville and Crofton. They were so far from their intended destination that the GPS constantly reoriented and recalculated the distance. Autumn gunned the engine once more, gained a little extra distance, and took the off-ramp. There was a small dip as she entered the ramp, which jolted the car upward. She lost control for a split second, eased on the brakes, and regained control.

The ramp wound upward and left. A large patch of trees obscured the view of the end of the ramp. She had been out this way many times before and knew what lay ahead. The traffic light directing the sparse traffic at the three-way stop was red on her approach. She cut hard right and merged onto the road toward Crofton. Farmland flanked both sides of the car as she settled into the two-lane road. Now only one option really remained: straight.

The truck followed behind, puffed out its wretched smoke, and followed them onto the unlit backroad.

Autumn rounded the first turn, which then hit a steep drop down a hill. Her stomach gave out for a moment—that split second tummy tickler people felt on roller coasters or airplanes—before eventually rising up and curving right again. The back roads were a dangerous place to be in a chase. No cover, nowhere to run. She had to get to the highway as soon as possible.

She saw several roadways toward farmland, but the truck was too close; it would see where they went. Turning to escape would mean getting boxed in, as the roads would eventually dead end. Autumn gripped the steering wheel at ten and two, steeled herself, and followed the road. She knew what was ahead, at least, which gave her an advantage.

The road branched into a four-way intersection. She knew she needed to turn left, as that would, after a couple miles, lead her to Route 50. As she approached the intersection, the light turned red for a left turn. She cursed, thought quickly, and slammed on the brakes. She turned right, followed the road for around fifty feet, then turned left into a gas station on the corner. The open space would give her the room she needed to move. The Honda popped the bump into the station, crossed through the collection of pumps, and skirted down the edge of a small parking area. At the end, a small opening led onto the road where they had come from. She glanced left and right, saw no traffic, and dashed out, turning left as she did. The truck still followed and traced her exact path.

In the intersection, on the opposite side, Autumn turned right and hit the gas pedal to head toward the outskirts of Crofton. After several miles, the road would divide again and lead to 50. They just had to survive till then.

Then, a bump from behind. Autumn and Cassie lurched forward.

Then another bump. They lurched again.

The truck was rearending the Honda, trying to force it off the road. The road had become a flat straightaway, with nowhere to run. Autumn mashed the gas pedal again and accelerated. Her eyes widened at a car turning onto the straightaway ahead. She dashed left into the oncoming lane and rounded the incoming car. The truck barreled through it and spun the incoming car sideways as it continued its advance.

The intersection to Route 50 was almost upon them. "Please be green. Please be green. Please be green," Autumn repeated as they approached. As their luck would have it, the light was red and crowded with cars at the stop. "Goddammit."

To the right, more small roads led to neighborhoods that would eventually cul-de-sac and trap them; to their left stood a small shopping center, with a wide-open and empty parking lot.

Autumn got as much distance as she could, pulled the hand brake, and turned the steering wheel hard to the left, popping the curb but getting them into a wide-open lot and out of traffic. As the car landed with a *thump*, she saw the truck do the same thing and follow their path. They circled around the lot, peeling and screeching their tires. A few pop-pop-pop sounds rang out as they continued their wide circle. More gunshots. The traffic light at the intersection finally turned green, and Autumn darted from the lot onto the road and blazed it as fast as possible toward the light. As she approached, it turned yellow. She prayed for time to stop for a split second and cut her just one break that night.

She passed through the yellow-turning-red traffic light and merged onto the road toward Route 50. The truck attempted to dart through the red light to catch up, but it was too late; it T-boned a tractor trailer. The truck folded in on itself, crumpled like a can, and came to a dead stop. The tractor trailer stopped in the middle of the intersection, which blocked traffic in every direction.

Autumn saw the devastation in her rearview mirror. She sighed and let her grip relax on the steering wheel. The Honda settled into a steady 50 mph and cruised toward Route 50.

Cassie, visibly shaken, sat forward. "Where'd you learn to drive like that?"

"DC. Washington DC." It wasn't a lie. Washington DC was considered one of the worst commutes in the United States, and the highways heading into the district converged with four driver locales: Maryland drivers, Virginia drivers, West Virginia drivers, and DC residents themselves, who all had their own quirks, attitudes, and styles of driving. But one thing was certain; put all of them in the same place at the same time, and it was a recipe for a commuting disaster. Traveling in the district had only one rule; be a bully or be bullied. There was no such thing as a "nice driver" in Washington DC. Autumn had made that commute so many times for work that she had grown used to it and knew all the best shortcuts and tactics to cut down on commute time. Though she hadn't been there for a while, the feeling of how to drive in the district and on its roads had returned like an old habit. It was serving her well that night.

The Honda merged onto the loop onto Route 50 toward Annapolis. Cassie sat back, shaking.

Autumn looked back. "You okay?"

Cassie started crying.

Autumn turned the heat to high and switched the radio to an oldies station. "Stuck in the Middle with You" by Stealer's Wheel was playing, and it felt oddly appropriate for the night. As they cruised down 50, they saw the tow truck, police cruisers, and EMS still cleaning up the mess from the earlier deer accident. No one seemed to notice the Honda passing in the opposite direction, and Autumn didn't bother to slow down to rubberneck the wreck.

She kept her pace steady at 55 mph all the way toward Annapolis, before circumnavigating to where they had started at the gas station in Edgewater.

Chapter Five

It was 10:15 p.m. The trucks hadn't returned, and Malcolm was becoming impatient. He sat in a reclining chair on the first floor of the bayside house, looking out the sliding glass door at the ink-dark Chesapeake Bay. It swayed and sloshed gently, calm in the winter night. Malcolm rocked forward and back, like the motion of an antique clock. Everything was riding on the latest shipment, and it had gone missing hours earlier from the basement.

Where the fuck are they?

A little less than an hour earlier, he had dispatched two of his best drivers to reclaim what was his. He had taken a risk with Max, giving him a second chance to prove his worth as a runner for shipments. But now, Max had burned his last piece of goodwill, cast his last stone, and shrugged off any chance of redemption. If Malcolm got his way, Max would be hanging upside down by his testicles in the living room of the bayside house right as the ball dropped in Times Square to ring in the new year.

And yet, the trucks still hadn't returned.

What should have been a short snatch-and-grab was long past its delivery date. Malcolm texted his most trusted driver, Cecil, for the fifth time.

No response. Not even a confirmation that Cecil had seen the message.

"Where the fuck are you?" he growled.

Finally, the phone rang.

"Cecil, you better have good news, or, in return, I'll have bad news for you."

"Sorry, Mal, we had a bit of a problem."

"What do you mean *a problem*? It's a tracked backpack in the hands of a moron junkie. What's the problem?"

Cecil groaned. "Well… it looks like the girlfriend took the bag and ran off in a car or something."

Malcolm stood and paced the room. The low lights cast a dim hue over the gloomy room. They only used the sparse house as a pickup point for distribution. No one lived there full time. "Well, here's a thought. Go get the girlfriend, whatever her fucking name is, and bring her and the stuff *here!* Why is that so hard to understand?"

"She didn't drive herself. I think she had someone pick her up. Then she tossed the tracer out the window."

"So… you lost her."

"Yeah. Sorry. We chased 'em, but the driver is really good. We went through Crofton but I hit a tractor trailer. Cops are here now."

"What *the fuck?* Where's Tobey?"

"He hit a deer on 50. Flipped over and a cop cruiser stopped for him. They probably have him in custody now."

"Please tell me you tossed your guns before the cops showed up."

Silence.

"*Fuck*," Malcolm screamed. He ran to the wall and punched the plaster repeatedly till he had blown a giant hole through it. "Everyone is a fucking moron!"

"Sorry, man. We didn't expect this. This driver, whoever it is, they're good."

"So, there's no way to track the package, you don't know where Max or his girlfriend are, and you and the other numb nuts are in police custody. Did I miss anything? Fill me in if there's something I don't know yet."

"I mean… that's basically been our night. We might need to get bailed out."

"You're my best driver, and now you've proven you're about as useful as an asshole on an elbow." Silence. Malcolm heard random chatter and sirens in the background on the line. "You'll get assistance soon. Don't worry."

"Thank, boss. I think they're about to take us in for questioning."

"That won't happen. Trust me." Malcolm hung up and dialed another number that he reserved for emergencies. The call rang twice, then went silent as the receiver answered. "Baskins, are you free tonight? I have an emergency, and you're the woman for the job."

******

POP!

"What was that?" Cassie yelled.

The car pulled to the right. The steering wheel jostled, and control became sluggish.

"It's a flat," Autumn said, slightly annoyed. "It's a flat, it's a flat, it's a flat."

The Honda pulled onto the shoulder of a dark road. They were the only car on the road, and the trees surrounded them like dark ghosts swaying slowly in the light breeze. Autumn stepped into the cold night and walked around to check which tire had blown—the front passenger side.

"Goddammit," she groaned. "This fucking night. I swear…" She trailed off into silence as she walked to the rear of the Honda, opened the trunk, lifted the cover, and retrieved the spare donut and car jack. As she approached the blown-out tire, Cassie stepped out, rubbing her arms to stave off the chilled night.

"You can stay in the car," Autumn said. "This will only take a second. The jack does the hard work." She slid the jack underneath the carriage, inserted the piston, and rotated it for elevation.

"I'm really sorry about tonight," Cassie said, shivering.

"Girl, if you say you're sorry one more time, I'll leave you on the side of the road, and I'll go out and enjoy my New Year's Eve at Castle Bay. Okay? Enough already!"

Cassie teared up and wept again. Autumn stopped spinning the jack, immediately regretting her words. They had come out harsher than she would have liked. She stood and embraced the ice-cold girl. Cassie wrapped her arms around Autumn and cried into her chest.

"I didn't mean for that to sound so… mean. I'm sorry."

"I'm… I'll pay you back for this. I promise." Cassie squeezed tighter for warmth.

Autumn sighed and released Cassie. "Come here." She went to the trunk to retrieve an extra hoodie that the cover had pushed into the back when she had raised it. She handed it to Cassie and resumed cranking the jack.

Cassie noticed the logo on the hoodie. "Didn't know you were a Commanders fan."

"I'm not," Autumn retorted. "It was my ex's. More of a Ravens fan."

Cassie slipped on the extra hoodie which made her look bulky. "What happened to your ex?"

Autumn stopped and regarded Cassie, who was bathed in the glow of the red taillights. "A little personal to ask your TAF driver, isn't it?"

"I'm… just making conversation."

Autumn was silent for a moment. "We're separated."

"What happened?"

"Nothing. And that's the reason." The car was finally raised all the way. Autumn took the crank for the jack, which doubled as a tire iron, and loosened the lugnuts of the blown-out tire's rim. She twisted them off and turned to Cassie. "Hey, come here. Make yourself useful. Hold these."

Cassie kneeled and extended her hands. A total of six large metal nuts landed in her frozen palms. She held them while Autumn lifted the spare like it had no weight at all. "You're strong," Cassie said.

"Gym and boxing. Keeps me occupied." She thought about Becky for a split second, then quickly brushed away the thought. *Not the time, not the place.* Autumn finished slipping the tire into place and, one by one, reset the nuts on their bolts, then tightened them with the tire iron. She cranked down the jack, and the new tire settled silently upon the road. "See? Nothin' to it. Let's go."

*****

Baskins, a quiet woman, spoke when she needed to and acted when she had to. In any other instance, she was a ghost. Sitting at the far end of a room, with her back to the wall, observing, noting, taking in the surroundings, she kept herself as plain and nondescript as possible— as forgettable as she could. Black hair, black clothes, black eyes. But when the time came to intermingle with crowds, like the flip of a switch, she could become a ball of laughter and joy, even if it was all for show.

Baskins had been diagnosed as a sociopath seven years ago and, in realizing her lack of emotional investment with others around her, had taken a liking to contract killing for local drug dealers in Annapolis and Baltimore and for crime families in the Washington DC area.

She enjoyed it. It fascinated her, watching people beg and sob when they knew their end was near. Something about the way they cried always seemed alien. Why did they always cry instead of just accepting it? The same thought was always fleeting though before she pulled the trigger on her silenced .45 caliber pistol. And like all her targets, they would eventually find their way into unmarked crab pots somewhere in the Chesapeake. She had forgotten how many lay on the muddy bottom, and she had long since lost track of where she had dumped them all.

Malcolm DeVries's call came in five minutes after she had sat to have a late dinner—a fast-food burrito, which suited her just fine. As she burned plenty of calories in her line of work, she was entitled to consume whatever she pleased without fear of gaining weight. As she ate, Malcolm said he needed her to complete a last— minute job as quickly as possible. Money was no object, which meant Baskins would charge triple.

She ate her burrito as she drove, turned on the police scanner under her dashboard, and listened for information regarding the location of Malcolm's drivers, Cecil and Tobey.

According to EMS, Tobey had been killed in a deer strike on Route 50. Cecil, however, was headed toward Anne Arundel Medical Center in the back of an ambulance. It had a cruiser as an escort, which meant the police would detain and guard Cecil upon arrival. Were they to interrogate him, it could expose Malcolm's entire operation.

Baskins would meet them halfway to handle the situation. She circled around through back roads before coming up Route 50. Using her GPS tracker, she followed the LoJack signal for Cecil's ambulance and found them headed on Route 50 toward Annapolis. They were nearing the exit to 665, which meant only a few minutes to spare.

Baskins hopped onto the opposite side of the highway and parked in the center of the off-ramp lane. She donned a black balaclava, retrieved her silenced pistol from the back seat, pulled the hood latch, and went to raise the hood. Baskins drove a black Ford Focus, a simple nondescript car that would never catch a gaze from any passerby—as boring as a contract killer would want to blend in and become unnoticeable.

As she pretended to fiddle with the engine, a flurry of red, white, and blue lights illuminated the area surrounding her car. She slid her gun hand deep into a crevice inside the engine and continued with the act.

Then a loud voice shouted, "Excuse me, please clear the road!"

"My engine stalled out," Baskins lied. "Could you help me?"

A twentysomething police officer stepped alongside her car. "Miss, you need to get your car off the road."

"You wanna help me? Stay exactly where you are."

In a flash, she pulled her hand from the crevice, tipped the barrel upward, and fired one-handed at the cop. His brain sprayed out the back of his head, and he fell backward like stack of wooden boards knocked down by a gust of wind. Baskins strode around the driver's side of the car. The EMS driver was panicking and shifting into gear as Baskins fired one shot into the driver's right temple. The ambulance slowly drifted forward and butted against the cruiser's left taillight with a loud *ka-chunk*. The taillight blew out and died immediately.

With a steady, even pace, Baskins approached the back of the ambulance and opened the rear doors. Inside were two paramedics and Cecil handcuffed to a gurney. Baskins lifted her pistol and fired two quick shots. Despite their panic, the paramedics went down quickly and crashed onto the cramped metal floor. She lowered her pistol and eyed Cecil.

Cecil smiled. "Oh, thank God. Malcolm must've sent you."

"Are you Cecil?" Baskin asked.

"Yeah."

"Good." She raised her gun again and fired.

Cecil went from uncontrollable joy to dead like a post in a split second. His brain sprayed the wall behind him and dribbled onto the gurney.

Baskins calmly closed the ambulance doors and drove away in her Ford Focus. A balaclava covered her face, her vehicle tags were fake, her gun and ammunition were unmarked and unregistered. There would be no traces. It was as if she didn't exist at all.

*****

Autumn's Honda cruised toward Edgewater. Cassie had moved to the front passenger seat, the backpack at her feet. Autumn gripped the steering wheel with her right hand and leaned on her left with her elbow propped on the window ledge. The night flowed by quietly. There was no music. Neither of them was in the mood.

Cassie watched the blur of dark shapes out the window while she contemplated what to do next. That backpack was her last chance at getting away from everything. But what if the dealer didn't accept it and killed her anyway? It was a risk, but she had no other choice. Someone, somewhere, would find her and end her. She swallowed hard at the thought that New Year's Eve could be her last night on Earth.

"When this is done, do you have anyone I can take you to?" Autumn asked.

"My mom lives in Pasadena," Cassie said. "You know where that is?"

"Yeah. I'll take you there when we're finished."

"Thanks." Cassie bit her fingernails.

"Stop that. It's a bad habit."

"Sorry."

Autumn sighed and increased the heater to the next level. The night was cold and only getting colder.

"Are you gonna message them again?" Cassie asked.

"Who?"

"Your ex. The one where nothing happened."

"I don't know."

"How long have you been separated?"

"Why do you care? It's none of your business."

Cassie lowered her head and went silent, like a scolded child

Autumn finally followed up with, "She and I split about three months ago."

"Oh. I think you should message her again. Just to at least say hi."

"Maybe."

"I might die tonight, so I'm just thinking about the things I would say to people if I really was sure I was gonna die."

"Life's short, kid. It goes by in a blink."

"It's not fair."

"I know."

"If we get through this okay, you should message her."

Autumn sighed as she said, "Let's get through the next hour. Then, if we're still breathing, go from there."

Cassie said nothing while she stared out the side window.

As the car rounded a bend on an unlit road, a pack of foxes sauntered across the road. Autumn eased on the brakes and came to a stop. The pack looked up at the car, their eyes glowing golden in the headlights. They stared for a second, then wandered across the road, slow at first, then sprinting.

As the foxes disappeared from the headlights, Autumn said, "Well, hope you make it." With the road clear, Autumn released the brakes and gently pressed the accelerator. They continued around the bend, leaving the foxes to their business.

*****

Fuck, fuck, fuck! Max thought. He tossed as many clothes as possible into a suitcase on his bed. He needed to get out of town, as far away as possible. Losing the fent would mean that DeVries would come for him soon.

Max had gotten greedy, had gotten stupid. He couldn't fight what might be coming for him. All he could do was run.

He removed all the cash from a small floor safe under a throw rug in the corner of the bedroom. It only added up to $30,000, but it was enough to start a small life somewhere else. Stay off social media, get a burner phone, work a dead-end job for a while—life would return to normal within six months. It was the only option he had left.

He tossed the cash into the suitcase and retrieved the case of spare .38 caliber rounds for his snub-nosed pistol. Best to be prepared. As he flipped the suitcase closed, Max felt a sharp pressure at the back of his neck. The barrel of a gun. He froze mid-zip on the suitcase.

"Open it back up," a woman said, flat and cold and emotionless.

Max obeyed, and the lid flopped open and landed on the bed with a soft *thunk.* The gun barrel slid around his neck and pressed into his right temple. He shut his eyes hard and shook, terrified. *Not fast enough*, he thought.

"I'm guessing you don't have the fent, huh?" the voice asked.

Max shook his head no.

"That's too bad. Take out the money and the gun."

He removed the wads of cash and the box of ammo, then reached to pull the snub-nose pistol from his black hoodie's right pocket.

"Slowly," the voice said sternly.

"I am going slowly," Max said, suppressing fear as best he could. He set the pistol on the bed next to the ammo case and raised his hands.

The woman who owned the voice moved around him again to collect the gun, ammo, and cash. She shoved the three items into her jacket pocket, then made a phone call. "I have Max. No fent though. Bring him to you or take care of it here?"

Max braced for the gunshot, slightly leaning away. He heard Malcolm on the other end of the line say, "No, bring him here. I want to handle it."

The woman hung up. "Well, it's your lucky day. You get an extra hour of life. Outside. To the car."

Max turned and walked out of the bedroom. The woman followed close behind yet far enough where he could not assault her. Whoever she was, she was very good. He hadn't even heard her enter the house. Only once they were outside in the cold did he realize he had pissed his pants.

Chapter Six

Autumn turned left onto Turkey Point Road—a sleepy road shrouded in darkness. From there, it was a straight shot to their destination. They passed a church on their left and a cemetery on their right. Autumn was never particularly religious despite her parents' upbringing. Even so, she hoped that passing a church and a graveyard on the way to her destination was not intended as a bad omen.

They came to a marina full of boats tarped and stacked in racks for the winter season, catching glimmers of the orange lamps that illuminated the marina. Once they had passed the marina, they crossed a small concrete bridge that marked the official start of the island.

Double yellow lines divided the thin and very flat two-lane road. Large two-story houses intermittently bordered each side, surrounded by that fake white fencing crap that an HOA could easily install—efficient but bland and a little cheap looking.

As the Honda kept a steady 40 mph, water eventually flanked the right side of the road. Ramsey Lake, which connected directly into the Chesapeake, seemed as if it was pressing in, struggling to gain an extra few feet of elevation, to finally overtake the road and reclaim the land for itself. The area was prone to flooding. Autumn thought, *You have to be a millionaire just to afford the insurance on these places.*

The land on the right finally returned, and they were on Turkey Point Island. Despite possibilities of flooding, it looked like a beautiful, quiet corner of the world. Random roads forked off the main thoroughfare, leading to cul-de-sacs and roundabouts, all of which featured gorgeous homes. Despite how dead the world seemed in the wintertime, Turkey Point felt like a bastion of positivity and a haven from the trouble of the Earth—a perfect place to hide a drop point for drug trafficking. No one would ever suspect a thing in such a lush setting.

The main road finally ended, and the double yellow lines vanished from the blacktop. No more streetlamps loomed overhead, and none of the houses had any lights on as they ventured into the farthest corner of the island. The landscape had changed. It was less clean, less polished. Untrimmed trees surrounded the road, which had an occasional pothole or divot.

As they reached the end of the road, Cassie pointed to a house on the right. "That's the one. Turn off your lights."

Autumn switched off her headlights and slowed to a crawl. As the street dead ended, she made a three-point turn and reversed direction. She pulled onto the right side of the road and parked. "Well, here we are," Autumn said with finality.

Cassie looked out Autumn's driver-side window at the two-story home sitting at the peak of a long-curved driveway. The house wasn't totally visible, as trees surrounded it and the driveway was gated. From what Autumn and Cassie could see, it was elegant and homely but nothing to denote any wrongdoing. It certainly wasn't the best-looking place on Turkey Point either. Vines grew across the fence in zigzag patterns, and the right swinging metal door of the driveway gate hung a bit low, signifying a lack of upkeep. Before they had arrived, Autumn assumed they could drop off the backpack on the front step and run. Now, seeing a gate and a long driveway, possibly watched by cameras or dogs or guards, or whatever else they might have, she wasn't sure what to do.

"Well, you wanna ring the bell, or should I?" Autumn asked.

Cassie said nothing as she lifted the backpack into her lap. The pack felt heavy as she considered her next move. Then she eyed Autumn. "This is worth seventy-five thousand dollars. We could run. And then—"

"Oh, goddammit!" Autumn yelled in frustration. She snatched the backpack from Cassie's lap and opened the car door.

Cassie tried to protest, but Autumn ignored her. Autumn strode to the gated driveway and searched for a bell in the darkness. "Fuck it." She reeled back and hurled the pack over the fence. It landed in the soft grass to the right of a willow tree, the vials inside clicking and clacking. She marched to the car and slammed the door as she sat down. "There. It's done."

Cassie began to speak but stopped herself. She felt ashamed of even considering keeping the pack. After everything that had happened, even presuming they could survive the night, someone would come after them. Throwing away the pack was the only sensible option.

Autumn leaned over to grab her phone. "What's your mom's address?"

Cassie recited the southern Pasadena, Maryland address. From Turkey Point, it would take forty to forty-five minutes to get there. At that time of night, there would be no traffic. Autumn entered the address into her GPS and secured her phone into its holder.

Neither of them spoke as they pulled away from the house, leaving the source of their trouble behind in the cold dead grass.

*****

"Stop crying," Baskins said flatly to Max, who had been on-and-off whimpering, as they cruised down the road.

Max knew his eventual fate was coming and could do nothing to stop it.

The Ford Focus was a simple vehicle and easy to maintain. Baskins liked its heated seats, internet connection for music, and all-wheel drive in case of snowstorms or heavy rain. It was also inexpensive, which she liked the most. As she drove, she became more annoyed with Max and his crying. Again, she wondered why people who had done wrong never just submitted to their punishment. Why beg? Why plead? Why was that so hard for anyone to understand?

To prevent Max from trying anything outrageous, heroic, or stupid, Baskins had zip tied Max's hands under his knees, which forced him to lean forward slightly. Amid one of her earliest hits, Baskins had been careless and did not properly secure her target during transport. The target had grabbed her steering wheel and flipped the car off the road to escape. Baskins's luck had held though, as the target wore no seatbelt, and the impact had deployed the airbag, which exploded into the right side of his head. He had been so close to the dashboard that the force snapped his neck, killing him instantly. Once the vehicle had stopped moving, she had bolted from the scene, leaving behind the dead body. Though technically a success, it had been sloppy, lazy, and unprofessional.

She would never make a mistake like that again.

The Focus came to a three-way stop on Central Avenue. The left turn would take her to Turkey Point Island and to Malcolm DeVries. As they slowed to a stop to let a triplet of random cars pass on Central, she noticed a Honda Accord had also stopped and had activated its right turn signal. In any other circumstance, she would think nothing of it. But that night, it seemed odd. *Nobody comes down here this late at night, especially on New Year's Eve.* She grumbled and tilted her head in confusion.

Max looked up, and his eyes widened. "That's her! That's them! They have the backpack!"

Without hesitation, Baskins pulled in front of the Accord. She flipped on her high beams to blind the driver and came to a stop, bumper to bumper. She retrieved her silenced pistol from under her seat, stepped into the cold night, and approached the Accord's passenger window. Inside were two women. One of them was Cassie; the other was a red-haired woman at the wheel. Baskins tapped the silencer on the glass. The window slowly lowered.

"Where is it?" Baskins asked calmly.

Cassie leaned away from the gun barrel aimed directly at her forehead. "It's back there. We threw it in the yard."

"Are you sure?"

"Yes. It's done."

"*Hmm.* Well, until I'm sure, I think you should turn around and go back."

The redhead leaned across the center console. "You got what you wanted. It's in the yard next to the tree. We don't—"

Baskins fired a round skyward. It zinged into the black above. Silencers, in real life, didn't sound like tiny *thwips*, like portrayed in movies or TV shows. They were still loud, just not loud enough to damage the shooter's eardrums—like a slightly muted thundercrack. Silencers were more for the operator than for the people on the business end of the barrel.

The redhead recoiled, and Cassie slinked lower in her seat.

"Both of you inconvenienced my night off," Baskins said.

"You're not the only one," the redhead murmured.

"Regardless, I have business with Mr. DeVries, and it involves ensuring I take care of loose ends. So, turn around and go back to the house." Baskins reached inside the passenger door, snatched a phone from a holder connected to the dashboard, then stuffed it into her pocket. She hit Unlock and opened the passenger door. She took a couple steps backward, still aiming at Cassie. "And as an incentive, you, girl, get in my car. Now. And you, whatever your names is—"

"Autumn."

"Autumn. Turn around and drive to the house."

Cassie sat frozen with fear.

Baskins shot another round, this time into the dirt. A puff of frozen earth shot up and landed on the floorboards of the car. "Last chance. Get out or—"

"I'm getting out! I'm getting out!" Cassie undid her seatbelt and stepped into the cold.

Baskins grabbed Cassie's arm and dragged her to the Focus, then shoved Cassie inside. Baskins collected the pack of zip ties from her trunk and did the same to Cassie as she had done to Max. When she was satisfied that Cassie was incapacitated, Baskins chucked the bag into the trunk and returned to Autumn's car. The passenger door was still open, and a *ding, ding, ding* was blaring. Baskins leaned into the car. "Don't be a hero. Turn around and lead the way back. I don't think I need to explain what will happen if you don't." Then she slammed the door shut.

Baskins slid into her driver's seat, holding the gun in her right hand and gripping the steering wheel with her left. Autumn's car reversed, then U-turned to head toward Turkey Point Island. Baskins smiled and fell in behind her. *What an excellent stroke of luck to ring in the New Year.*

*****

As she drove back the way she had come, Autumn thought, *Just my fucking luck again. I should have read my horoscope this morning.*

CHAPTER SEVEN

utumn, Cassie, and Max, with their hands zip tied, kneeled on the back patio of the bayside house. A harsh patio light shone on them and cast long dark shadows in the direction of the Chesapeake. Baskins stood a few feet behind them, gun gripped firmly in her right hand. In front of the trio of prisoners, Malcolm inventoried each vial of fentanyl from the backpack in groups of five to keep tally and set them on the stone patio. As he quietly counted them to himself, a small propellered plane flew overhead toward Lee Airport—a small private airstrip that shipped his supply all over the state.

Tonight, though, it was just another plane—the lone sound in the night, besides the small *tink tink tink* of the fent vials when he set them upon the stone.

Then Malcolm stopped. He removed shards of glass from the backpack. Three vials had broken, and clear fluid had seeped out and coated the inside of the backpack.

Autumn closed her eyes hard and mentally kicked herself. *You should have just set it at front of the gate, you idiot.*

Max saw the damage and trembled. Cassie shook from fear and the cold, being the least prepared for the winter weather.

Malcolm finished counting and had pulled more than ninety variable sizes of fent vials from the backpack—minus the three destroyed ones, which still meant the backpack could generate over $70,000 in profit. Even so, Malcolm furrowed his brow and scowled hard at the trio of prisoners kneeling before him. A greedy employee, his addict girlfriend, and a random driver had ruined his whole night. It was enough stress to give anyone a stomach ulcer.

Malcolm carefully collected the broken fent vials and approached Max. Malcolm towered over him and breathed in and out, slowly, his breath projecting from his nostrils like a dragon ready to release scorching hot flames. Max didn't move; he just kept staring at the ground.

Malcolm kneeled and raised the glass shards to Max's face. "You see this? This is because of you. All roads tonight lead back to you, you fucking piece of shit. You thought you could steal from me? Did you? *Did you?*"

Max started crying again.

Malcolm stood, walked a few paces away, then reeled around and chucked the shards at Max. They scattered everywhere but landed harmlessly. Max recoiled, then resumed crying quietly.

Baskins walked over to Malcolm and pulled Max's $30,000 from her jacket pocket. "I think this will more than cover lost income for you."

Malcolm took the cash and ran the crisp, fresh bills through his fingers—probably had just been put into circulation. He cocked an eyebrow, satisfied with himself, then he grunted in disgust at Max. "All right. Do it."

Baskins circled the trio and stood before Max. Her gun was like a cold lump of black ice in her hand. She thumbed back the hammer. "Look at me."

Max kept crying uncontrollably.

"Look. At. Me."

Finally, with tears and snot streaking his face, Max looked up at Baskins.

"Good boy." Baskins casually raised her gun, aimed at Max's forehead, and fired.

The bullet ripped through his brain and sprayed the stone patio behind him like a Jackson Pollock painting. His eyes went blank, and he crumpled forward. His face slammed into the stone with a wet *thud*.

Cassie wretched forward and puked. Autumn turned away in terror and realized that if she didn't make a move soon, she would be next. *Think, goddammit. Think!*

Baskins eyed Max's lifeless body and said to no one, "Why do they always cry? So weird." She grabbed the spent shell casing and slid it into her jacket pocket.

As Malcolm slowly packed up the vials of fent, Baskins asked, "Same for them?"

"Yeah. Then use the boat on the dock to get rid of them."

"All right."

"I know where you can get more," Autumn blurted out.

Malcolm and Baskins turned and faced Autumn.

"What?" Malcolm asked.

"I know where you can get more."

"Where?"

"Let her go, and I'll take you to it."

"You're full of shit."

"My ex works at Anne Arundel Medical Center. She's a nurse. She can get as much as you want. Tonight. Replace your lost inventory."

"She's lying," Baskins interjected.

"Am I? How do you know? You're crazy."

Baskins said nothing, just stood statue-like, leering at Autumn.

Malcolm stepped over and leaned down over Autumn. "I want to believe you, but I just think you're full of shit. However, to make sure, I'll have Baskins here take a run at you, get you to talk truth." He stood upright and faced Baskins. "Take them downstairs and see what she says. Take the girl too. Maybe she called someone. Find out what they know and who they might have talked to."

Baskins pulled Autumn to her feet, then did the same to Cassie. She pushed them together and forced them into the dark house, her gun aimed at their lower backs. If they tried to run, a bullet through the spine would paralyze them but not kill them instantly. Torture would still be in order.

The trio moved through the house, down a hallway, and finally to a brown wooden door that led to the basement.

"Step back," Baskins said.

Autumn and Cassie backed up against the wall as Baskins opened the basement door, then flicked her gun barrel toward the entryway. As they descended the stairs, Baskins flipped on the lights to reveal a clean and efficient den filled with three tables in the middle, containing rows of various drugs, such as cocaine, heroin, and, of course, fentanyl. Several stacks of cash were lined up in neat columns. To the left side sat a thin metal table that featured a large electronic safe with a front-facing keypad. The opposite side of the room boasted a gun rack with a selection of standard assault rifles and a set of handguns below them. The room was extraordinarily well maintained despite being the hub of operations. Not a mark on the floor. The room had no odor beyond the typical basement mildew smell.

Baskins jammed the barrel of her gun into Cassie's lower back. "Keep moving."

Cassie butted against Autumn as Baskins pushed them through the room toward the back wall, where a complete map of Maryland hung. Baskins slid around the pair of women and pulled away the bottom edge of the poster to reveal a small black handle. Baskins flipped the handle downward, and a secret door that encompassed the entire poster opened.

"In," Baskins ordered.

The pair obeyed.

Baskins followed and closed the door behind them.

*****

The torture room was clean. No smell in the air at all. Freshly scrubbed tiles, washed walls, a large sink in the back. Several wooden chairs lined the left-hand wall where the trio entered. The ceiling contained a small air duct for ventilation and a fan that was nowhere near as well maintained as the rest of the room.

Baskins flipped a switch on the wall to the left of the door, and the fan revved up with a low humming, then eventually settled into a sluggish spin, with a slight squeak on every other rotation. A table that held multiple instruments—rope, a scalpel, a wrench, a hatchet, a three-foot length of barbed wire alongside a pair of gloves, and a pair of alligator clamps connected to a car battery—sat beside a small circular grated drain in the floor.

"Sit," Baskins ordered.

Autumn and Cassie sat together in the wooden chairs against the wall. Baskins silently glared at them. Autumn stared right back. Cassie dropped her head and whimpered in fear.

"One chance. Who else did you contact tonight?" Baskins asked.

"No one," Cassie responded, seemingly speaking to the floor.

Baskins grunted as the squeaking of the overhead fan seemed incredibly loud in the enclosed space. Baskin holstered her gun and faced the table. "It's a forgone conclusion that torture doesn't actually provide any useful information. During the second war in Iraq, we used torture to get as much out of anyone as we could, whether they were guilty of a crime or not." She grabbed the scalpel and examined it. "After a while, we saw that it was bullshit. Threaten to cut a man's balls off or to give a woman a forced hysterectomy, and they'll tell you where the Dead Sea Scrolls are buried. They'll tell you where to find the body of Jesus Christ. Or who they talked to during a very long New Year's Eve night." She put down the scalpel and refocused on the pair. "So, last chance. Who did you contact between the hours of nine p.m. and now? Name names, and I'll see about cutting you loose."

Fucking lies. She's gonna kill us no matter what. Autumn thought hard about what to do. Last chance to get out. Last chance to make things right. She was scared, more scared than she had ever been. She was a tough woman, but that didn't exactly equal brave. She had to pee really bad and wanted to go home. This wasn't where she wanted to die—in a dismal basement torture room surrounded by strangers.

The only option left was spontaneity.

"Okay," Autumn said.

"Okay, what?" Baskins said.

"I'll bring up the name and address of the person I called tonight. His name is Jeff," Autumn lied. "I'll give you everything you need to know. I don't know him really well, so I'll trade his life for mine. Does that work for you?"

Baskins was silent for a moment, then she folded her arms. "Fine. Tell me."

"It's in my phone."

Baskins retrieved Autumn's phone and attempted to open it. It was locked.

"It has two-point verification on it. Needs my face and thumbprint."

Baskins handed the phone to Autumn. "Open it. And don't bother trying to get a signal down here."

Autumn pressed her thumb to the screen and held the phone to eye level. In truth, she only needed the thumbprint to unlock her phone. Stealthily, she opened her camera settings and aimed it at Baskins while pretending to struggle with the facial tracking. "One sec. It's scanning now. Almost done." Then she activated the flash.

A brilliant flash of light blinded Baskins for the split second Autumn needed. Autumn leaped from her chair and piledrove into Baskins stomach. The pair slammed into the table and knocked the tools onto the floor. Autumn rammed herself into Baskins stomach while desperately reaching for something, anything, to use as a weapon. Baskins fought back, straining to draw her firearm from her holster inside her coat. As she finally drew it, the swipe of a wrench knocked it from her hand.

Autumn was finally armed, and despite being zip tied, she could still fight. Baskins kicked Autumn in the stomach, twirled around, and snatched the hatchet from the floor as Cassie cowered into the corner, away from the brawl. The pair of fighters circled each other, each one waiting for the other to make a move.

Baskins moved around and blocked the exit door. "Only way out is through me."

"You fucking psychotic bitch. Just shut up and try to fucking hit me."

Baskins, unfazed, lunged forward with a swipe, left to right. Autumn dodged backward and returned a swipe of her own. Both missed their targets.

They stalked around the room a bit more, each one occasionally glancing at the silenced pistol on the floor. Whoever got ahold of that would be victorious by default. And so, the circle around the room continued. Autumn took a slice across her right thigh; Baskins took a harsh blow to her left forearm, shattering the bone in her dominant side. Baskins stumbled away in pain, clearing the path to the door.

Seeing the advantage, Autumn flung open the door and faced Cassie. "Cassie, get up and ru—"

Baskins speared her body into Autumn, shoving them back into the drug den. She brandished the scalpel in her right hand. As they hit the floor, Baskins reeled back her arm to make a plunging attack on Autumn.

Autumn resisted, sliding herself along the floor, as Baskins straddled her. Baskins plunged down, but Autumn raised her arms to grasp the wrench in both hands and block the incoming blade. Caught in a deadlock, the two brutal women stared each other down.

Anger and rage filled Baskins. It would take weeks to fix such a devastating blow to her arm. Meanwhile, Autumn was just terrified and fighting for her life.

Autumn pushed back with all her might and shoved Baskins upward. Autumn's arms were burning. She was exhausted. She could only muster one last bit of power to finish the fight. She dug deep and shoved Baskins upward till she was sitting upright while straddling Autumn.

Then, a loud bang.

Baskins stomach exploded as a bullet burst through her lower spine. Still alive but paralyzed, she collapsed forward and landed on Autumn's chest.

Autumn craned her head to peer over Baskins's body. Cassie stood in the doorway, brandishing the silenced pistol.

"I can't move," Baskins said calmly. "This is so weird. I can't move."

Autumn flipped Baskins paralyzed body off her and got up. Baskins had landed face up, unable to move. Autumn kneeled and grabbed the scalpel to cut her bonds, then did the same for Cassie. "Let me have that."

Cassie relented and handed the gun to Autumn.

"I'm moving, aren't I?" Baskins asked. "I'm telling my body to move. It's moving, right?"

She didn't move.

Autumn stood high over Baskins's frozen body, gun aimed at her, then noticed the large and heavy electronic safe on the metal table. Autumn smiled, tossed the gun onto the table, then dragged Baskins toward the safe.

"What are you doing?" Baskins asked.

Autumn positioned Baskins's head below the safe's position, then glared at Baskins. "You wanna know why they were crying?" She grasped the back edge of the safe. "Because they were scared, you fucking cunt!"

With all her might, she pulled the safe forward. It slowly began to topple. Then it fell.

"*Noooooooooo*—" The safe smashed Baskins's head like a grapefruit.

Autumn and Cassie stood quietly in the den, still processing what had happened in the last few minutes. Finally, Autumn retrieved her phone from the torture room. The screen had a small crack, but it was still functional. She shoved it into her pocket and headed into the den, where Cassie stared at Baskins's headless body. Autumn thought Cassie had done nothing to deserve this. She had made some mistakes, sure, but this was too far. Someone had to pay.

Then she surveyed the piles of cash on the table and smirked.

Autumn searched the room for anything to use as a bag. She eventually found a red backpack, not too dissimilar from the fentanyl-filled backpack from earlier. Autumn opened it and saw it was empty. She rushed to the table to scoop up every stack of cash, then zipped the bag closed and handed it to Cassie. "To start a new life."

Cassie accepted the bag, then lunged forward to hug Autumn.

Autumn gave in and lightly hugged back. "All right, that's enough. Time to go."

As they headed out, Cassie said, "Hey, you've got red on you."

Autumn spotted herself in a wall-hanging mirror and saw blood covering her face and chest. She headed into the torture room to wash her face in the sink. Not much she could do about her hoodie, but the red of the blood blended well enough with the red of the Maryland Terps design on the front.

******

Malcolm stood on the patio, smoking a joint, while watching the night sky. Max's dead body had been slid toward the wall, out of the way, waiting for Baskins to come upstairs to finish the job. The backpack of vials lay beside Max's body.

It was five minutes till midnight. Every New Year's Eve, a boat in the Annapolis harbor set off fireworks in celebration. He was ready to ring in the new year on a good note.

Then, behind him, he heard the sliding glass door open to the house. "They finally talk?" Malcolm asked. Then he felt the barrel of a gun press into the back of his head.

"You mean did *Baskins* talk?" Autumn asked. "You see, you need a head for that. She doesn't really have one anymore."

"Oh, fuck," Malcolm whispered in terror. The joint hung on for dear life from his lips.

"*Mm-hm*. My keys. Where are they?"

"My right pocket."

Cassie began to walk around Autumn to take the keys, but Autumn stopped her. "What?"

"He'll try to grab you if you reach into his pocket. Turn around!"

Malcolm slowly turned and saw the gun barrel aimed at his forehead.

"All right," Autumn said. "Strip."

"What?" Malcolm asked, taken aback.

"Down to your bare ass. Cassie, do me a favor. Go into the garage and see if there's some gasoline. Something flammable."

Cassie obliged and headed to the garage.

Malcolm slowly peeled away his clothing, piece by piece—his jacket, shirt, shoes, and pants. Finally, he was only clothed in his socks and underwear.

"That thirty-K you had. Where's that?" Autumn asked.

Through chattering teeth, Malcolm responded, "Left… pocket."

Autumn retrieved her keys and the $30,000 from Malcolm's jacket. She shoved them into her hoodie and stood upright.

Cassie returned with a can full of gasoline. "Okay, now what?"

"Dump it all over the house. And you"—Autumn refocused on Malcolm—"I said to your bare ass."

"Oh, come on!" Malcolm pleaded.

"Do it!"

Malcolm slipped off his socks and boxer shorts and stood completely exposed to the excruciating December night. Cassie looked at Malcom's groin and saw something extremely small that made her giggle.

"On brand for this guy, huh?" Autumn asked.

"Definitely," Cassie agreed.

Cassie returned inside and dumped slosh after slosh of gasoline all over the house. The fumes were pungent and found their way outside through the patio door.

Autumn snatched the still-smoking joint from Malcolm's mouth and took a long, heavy drag. She puffed out a smoke ring as Malcolm shivered and held himself in the cold.

From inside there was a loud *thunk*. "All done?" Autumn asked.

"All done," Cassie replied.

"Good, grab his clothes."

Malcom pleaded as Cassie silently collected all his clothes.

"Now get the tent."

Cassie snatched the backpack from next to Max's corpse. She considered saying a few words, something malicious, something hateful, something that would firmly put a stamp on what she had endured with him, but all she could manage was a "Fuck you," then she spit in his face. Cassie slung the backpack over her shoulder and stepped behind Autumn.

Malcolm was in extreme pain, the cold of the night gnawing at him, trying to sap every ounce of heat from his body. All he could do was stand in place and shiver. Through chattering teeth that seemed on the verge of shattering, he asked, "Who *the fuck* are you?"

"Me?" Autumn asked. "Just a Good Samaritan."

Fireworks exploded in the distance. The harbor, a few miles away, lit up like a liquid Christmas tree and rippled in the night. Bang after bang, burst after burst, the night sky strobed, ringing in the New Year.

Autumn pulled the joint from her mouth and glanced into the house. "Happy fucking New Year." Then she flicked the still-lit joint onto the gasoline-soaked rug.

"*Nooooooooooo!*"

The interior of the house lit up gloriously and became of beacon in the night. Everything inside would burn to ash.

Autumn and Cassie circled Malcolm, who no longer paid attention to them. He was more concerned with the loss of his base of operations. Were he to live through the night, it would be impossible to restart. *So much product! Wasted!*

"I wouldn't walk too far from the fire," Autumn said. "It's cold out tonight."

The pair maneuvered around the house, down the driveway, and to Autumn's car. Autumn pulled an extra T-shirt—one of her ex's—from the trunk and wrapped it around the slice on her leg, wincing from the pain. The duo slid into the front seats and looked behind them to watch the house burn.

"We should leave before firetrucks show up," Cassie said.

"Yeah, that's probably a good idea."

Autumn started the engine, fired up the heater to full blast, and gunned it from Turkey Point Island. The fire in the rearview mirror was a sight unto itself.

As they sped down the road, Cassie opened her passenger window to chuck out vial after vial of fentanyl. Once she had emptied the bag, she bellowed a raucous yell, feeling free of Max, Malcolm, Baskins, and everything of that night. Autumn did the same, chucking Baskins's gun out the window as they crossed the bridge to leave the island.

Autumn turned on the radio and flipped through her playlists. She eventually landed on "Everybody Have Fun Tonight" by Wang Chung. The two ladies danced and sang to their victory as they cruised toward southern Pasadena.

The midnight fireworks continued for the next fifteen minutes, illuminating the road ahead.

CHAPTER EIGHT

Cassie rang the doorbell. Her mother answered in her red bathrobe. The girl leaped forward and embraced her mother. Autumn stood at the front of the porch and watched. When they had arrived, Autumn had removed her blood-covered hoodie and reclaimed her ex's Commanders hoodie, while secretly transferring the wad of cash from one pocket to another. Cassie would just have to endure a few minutes of cold.

"I'm sorry, Mom," Cassie said. "Can I come home?"

"Oh my God, yes. My baby." Cassie's mother hugged her daughter so hard that it almost hurt.

"Well, it's been a long night," Autumn said, trying her best to not break the mood. "I'm gonna, you know, scoot."

"No, wait." Cassie's mother approached Autumn to shake her hand. "Are you her friend?"

"Eh, more like *friendly*. I was her driver tonight."

"Her driver?"

"Long story. She'll tell you about it tomorrow. Just take care of her."

"She ran off with that awful boyfriend months ago. Thank you for bringing her home."

"Just doing my job. I'm gonna go. Happy New Year."

"Hey!" Cassie ran to Autumn and hugged her again.

Autumn committed to the hug, enjoying the warmth of another person against her skin. It had been so long since she had felt such kindness.

"Thanks for tonight."

Autumn remembered the 30K in her pocket and smiled. "Of course. And thanks for the tip." Then she turned and walked toward her car.

Cassie raised an eyebrow and said to herself, "Tip?"

But before she could ask, Autumn was already in the car and peeling away down the road.

*****

Autumn rolled casually down the road. She kept the heater high and the radio on a Top 40 station. As she stopped at a stoplight, she checked the time—12:45 a.m., which meant last call at all the bars, which also meant a bunch of pickups and drop-offs. Despite making a pretty penny, and all the bullshit of the night, she hovered her finger over the TAF app icon. "Eh, what the hell? What's one more?"

Right as she signed in, she got a hit for a pickup. The passenger was the same as her first one of the night—Trevor.

She headed toward Annapolis and, like many other TAF drivers, stopped in front of Stan and Joe's Tavern, then remembered the bullet hole in her trunk. She scolded herself for forgetting, but it was too late to do anything about it. She just hoped no one noticed.

The rear passenger door opened and in slid a very inebriated Trevor and an even more inebriated Maggie. Trevor recognized her immediately. "Hey, hey, Autumn! Good to see you back again!"

"Yep, back again. You have fun tonight?"

"Oh, it was so much fun," Maggie said, doing her best to not slur her words. "Why can't they do this every weekend?"

"Because New Year's Eve only happens once a year." Autumn merged into the roadway toward Route 50.

"Did you have a good night, at least? Lots of tips?" Trevor asked.

Autumn reached down and felt the 30K resting in her hoodie pocket. "Eh, it was pretty good, all things considered."

The Honda merged onto Route 50, and Autumn raced down the road to take the drunken pair home.

*****

The next day, Autumn didn't wake up till noon. She was beaten, battered, bruised. All the *B*s, including bloated, as that morning, she got her period. "Just my fucking luck," she said to herself. As she cleaned herself, she inspected her injuries in the reflection of the mirror. She cleaned the slice on her leg and did her best to wrap it. She would need to see a doctor for stitches probably, but, for now, it could wait. Her back and arms were bruised as well from the fight with Baskins. Thinking about Baskins made her skin crawl. *How does someone become like that?*

After cleaning up and putting in a tampon, she fixed herself a pot of coffee and sat in her living room to listen to some soft music on YouTube. Even though she had just woken up, she felt as though she could sleep for a thousand years.

Autumn stood and fought through the pain in her leg to walk to her hoodie. She removed the $30,000, plopped it on the table, and smiled. Yeah, it had been worth it. Doing a good deed was one thing. Doing a good deed and getting paid handsomely for it, that was a nice bonus. She reached back into her hoodie to get her phone. She expected to see a message from Cassie or from someone who would come knocking, expecting an explanation for the previous night, but nothing. No messages.

No one had even messaged her a *Happy New Year.*

Seeing how empty her notifications were, she felt a little sad and lonely.

Autumn walked to the window to look at the parking lot below. Her car could be easily seen, and the bullet hole was even more egregious in the daylight. The 30K would easily cover that and leave a bunch left over.

As she sipped her coffee, Autumn recalled the conversation she'd had with Cassie when they had been driving to Turkey Point Island—Cassie's existential moment, contemplating what she would say to people if she knew she was going to die. She'd implored Autumn to contact her ex, say something, try to do better.

They'd survived the night. Now she had to live up to that expectation.

Autumn opened her messages and pulled up the last thread between her and Becky. She paused, unsure what to say. Should it be something apologetic, something funny, explain what had happened last night?

Finally, she landed on: *Happy New Year. I miss you.*

Then she closed her phone.

As she took another sip of her coffee, her phone pinged.

BECKY: *Happy New Year! I miss you too.*

Autumn smiled and cried happy tears.

New year, new me.

ABOUT THE AUTHOR

Born in the suburbs of Maryland in 1985, Jesse Fresco began writing as an escape from his day job as a stagehand. His work is heavily inspired by his sixteen years in the film industry and various life experiences. An avid reader with a library of over four hundred prose novels and graphic novels, he found inspiration in the works of Garth Ennis, Lee Child, Derek Robinson, and Stephen King. He currently lives in Davidsonville, Maryland with his family.

To get in contact with the author, go to
http://www.instagram.com/jessefresco
https://www.facebook.com/jessefresco
https://www.threads.com/@jessefresco
https://x.com/HardCoreBShot